Lost In The Woods . . .
At Night!!!

"A scavenger hunt is a stupid idea! And in the *woods*—of all places!" Tanya winced.

"But you can't go back! We'll lose," wailed Missy.

"You don't need me as a partner. And you don't need a compass either." Tanya tucked the compass into the pocket of her shorts and headed back in the direction they had come.

Missy jumped up. "You're not going anywhere," she said. "And certainly not with my compass!"

Tanya turned around. "Try and stop me," she taunted.

Missy lunged at Tanya, grabbing her around the waist. They both fell to the ground.

Then they heard it—a horrible crunching sound. Tanya had fallen on the compass!

D1400232

MEET MISS DRACULA

by Molly Albright

illustrated by Dee deRosa

Troll Associates

Library of Congress Cataloging in Publication Data

Albright, Molly.
   Meet Miss Dracula.

   Summary: Though she tries hard to be friendly
and understanding, twelve-year-old Missy finds it
difficult to get along with her sophisticated cousin from
New York.
   [1. Cousins—Fiction.   2. Behavior—Fiction.   3. Family
life—Fiction.   4. Dogs—Fiction]   I. deRosa, Dee, ill.
II. Title.
PZ7.A325Me   1988   [Fic]   87-13871
ISBN 0-8167-1157-7 (lib. bdg.)
ISBN 0-8167-1158-5 (pbk.)

A TROLL BOOK, published by Troll Associates,
Mahwah, NJ 07430

Printed in the United States of America.

10 9 8 7 6 5 4 3 2 1

MEET MISS DRACULA

CHAPTER 1

Baby's ears perked up. Sometimes strangers had a hard time finding his ears under all his hair, but Melissa Fremont noticed immediately. Baby was Missy's huge Old English sheepdog and her very best friend.

"Look, Dad," said Missy. "It's Baby's favorite commercial."

On TV, another Old English sheepdog was barking to a rock beat. Behind him a rock band of sheepdogs wearing sunglasses looked like they were singing.

My coat was dull and full of fleas,
So I went to the store and said, "Pretty please,
Give me some Doggie Yum-Yums!
Now I look like a Yum-Yum doggie!"

Baby's tail thumped in time to the musical barking.

Mr. Fremont laughed. "Maybe we can get Baby

an audition. You know my sister, Jessica, wrote that ad. She told me about it when I was in New York with the symphony last winter." The Fremonts lived in Indianapolis. Mr. Fremont played first viola with the Indianapolis Symphony.

Missy turned to her father. "How come I have an aunt I've never met?"

"Well, Jessica moved to New York when she was very young, and then she got married. She and I never stayed close," said Mr. Fremont thoughtfully. "Actually, she's got a daughter just your age." Missy was twelve.

"Jessica sounds neat," said Missy. "Maybe that's what I'll be when I grow up—a jingle writer. I can see it all now. . . . My glamorous aunt in New York will give me my first big break."

Missy patted Baby's coat, which looked pretty glossy even without Doggie Yum-Yums.

"Baby deserves a chance to make it big on TV too," Missy said. She leaned down and gave him a hug. She knew that Baby was the best-looking and smartest sheepdog in the world. He was enormous now, but when Missy chose him, he had been just a little ball of fur. Missy's parents had often told Missy that when they adopted her as a tiny baby, they had fallen in love with her at first sight. When Missy first saw Baby, she had fallen in love with him too.

It was Baby who had comforted Missy when the Fremonts first moved to Indianapolis from Cincinnati the year before. It had taken Missy a while to get used to a new city and school and to make new friends. But Baby was always there when Missy needed him, just like a best friend should be. In fact, the Fremonts always said that Missy and Baby were two of a kind.

Missy gave Baby a kiss and started to sing.

Hey, Baby, Doggie Yum-Yums are mighty fine,
But I like chocolate some of the time.

Mr. Fremont groaned. "I don't think we should do anything to encourage Baby's love of chocolate."

"What's this I hear about chocolate?" asked Mrs. Fremont as she came into the living room, carrying a big bowl of popcorn.

"Missy has new career plans," said Mr. Fremont. "She wants Jessica to get her started in the jingle-writing business."

"Poor Jessica," said Mrs. Fremont.

"Why do you say that?" asked Missy. "She's got the greatest job in the world. And she gets to live in New York City. I think her life sounds neat."

"Yes, but she's getting divorced," said Mr. Fremont. "It must be tough on her and on her daughter."

Missy bit her lip. Although many of her friends' parents were divorced, she felt sorry for the cousin she had never met. She hoped "divorce" would never happen to her folks.

"Maybe we should invite them here for a visit," said Missy.

Mr. and Mrs. Fremont looked at each other. "You know, Missy, that's a very nice idea," said Mr. Fremont. "Jessica and I talked about trying to get our families together. It seemed a little sad that you and Tanya had never met."

"Tanya. Is that my cousin's name?" Missy asked.

Mr. Fremont nodded. "Tanya Rosoff."

"It might be just what Jessica and her daughter need," said Mrs. Fremont. "Indianapolis would be a quiet retreat, and Tanya and Missy are just the same age—they'd probably have a great time together."

"And we could give them some good home cooking, like Dad's special spaghetti sauce," said Missy. "That would make anybody feel better."

"Okay, I'll call her right now," said Mr. Fremont. He looked at his watch. "It must be just about dinnertime in New York."

Missy's father reached for the phone. Missy patted Baby. "This may be our lucky night," she whispered into Baby's ear. "I'll bet when Aunt Jessica sees *you*, she'll want you to replace that lead dog. And when she meets *me*, she'll want me to be her assistant right away."

Missy listened as her father talked on the phone. He seemed to be mostly grunting "Uh-huh," with an occasional "Oh, really?" sprinkled with an "Oh, no" or two.

"Have you ever met Aunt Jessica?" Missy asked her mother.

"Just once, at our wedding," said Mrs. Fremont. "I thought she was a little bit—um, weird."

"What was so weird about her?" Missy asked curiously.

"Well, for one thing, she had bright red hair with purple streaks. It was so short, it was nearly a crew cut," said Mrs. Fremont. "And this was before punk fashions got popular."

"I think that's great. She sounds like a real fashion trendsetter," said Missy admiringly. She glanced into the hall mirror at her mop of curly

red hair, wondering what she'd look like with a crew cut.

"She also wore blue cowboy boots to our wedding. As I recall, the boots had five-inch heels."

"She's definitely going to stand out in Indianapolis," said Missy. "I can't wait to meet her. Maybe she'll take me shopping."

"Not unless I go along," said Mrs. Fremont with a slight shudder.

Mr. Fremont hung up the phone. He had a slightly puzzled expression on his face.

"Well, are they coming?" asked Mrs. Fremont.

"Not *they*," said Mr. Fremont slowly. "*She* . . ."

"What does that mean?" demanded Missy.

Mr. Fremont sighed. "Well, Jessica was thrilled that I called. She has a chance to go to Europe this summer, and she can't take Tanya with her. So she asked if Tanya could stay with us for three weeks. She said that she thought Tanya would 'cool out' in Indianapolis."

"What does *that* mean?" asked Mrs. Fremont.

Mr. Fremont shrugged. "I gather Tanya's a little angry about the divorce."

"But I wanted to meet Aunt Jessica, the jingle writer," wailed Missy. "Who knows what her daughter's like? She could be a creep. Where's she going to sleep?" Missy asked suspiciously.

"She'll have to share your room," said Mrs. Fremont thoughtfully. "I hope she doesn't find Indianapolis too boring after New York. Did you meet Tanya in New York?"

Mr. Fremont shook his head. "Jessica and I just met for lunch one day."

"You mean, I'm going to have to entertain a

perfect stranger for three weeks?" asked Missy. "Someone nobody in this whole family has ever met?"

"Missy," warned Mrs. Fremont. "Remember, this whole thing was your idea."

"I know, but you didn't have to take me up on it so fast," said Missy.

Mrs. Fremont laughed. "Come on, Missy. It was a very sweet and thoughtful idea. I'm sure we'll all learn to love Tanya. After all, she's family."

CHAPTER 2

Missy tugged on Baby's leash. "Come on, we have to go inside now," she told him. But Baby refused to move. He sat down right in the middle of the automatic doorway of the airport. Baby hated airports. He had a good memory and could remember his last trip to an airport. He had been put in a box and had to fly in the cargo compartment.

"We're not taking you on a plane," promised Missy as the door in front of them flapped open and shut. Passengers trying to get around Baby looked down in amusement.

"Come on, we're going to miss Tanya," Missy pleaded.

Baby did not look interested. He lay down. Missy put her hands under Baby's stomach and tried to lift him. Baby went limp.

"Mom, Dad, help!" cried Missy.

Mr. Fremont took Baby's front paws and Mrs. Fremont his back. With Missy carrying the middle, they managed to get him through the doorway and onto the escalator.

"I think we should have left Baby at home," puffed Mrs. Fremont.

"Oh, no," cried Missy. "I'm sure Tanya will like Baby. Everybody likes Baby. Even if she doesn't like us, she'll like Baby."

"Missy, don't worry," said Mrs. Fremont. "Tanya will like you, with or without Baby."

"I know, but Baby is a good insurance policy," said Missy.

With a combination of begging and pushing, they got Baby to the gate.

Missy told Baby to sit. She unrolled a sign she had made and hung it around Baby's neck. Missy had decorated the sign with flowers and hearts, and had written WELCOME, COUSIN TANYA! on it.

"There," said Missy as she straightened the sign. "Okay, Baby, don't move until Tanya gets here."

Baby lay down, crumpling the sign underneath him.

"Oh, no," cried Missy.

"Don't worry," said Mrs. Fremont. "It's the thought that counts. Look, the passengers are coming out."

"Sit up," Missy told Baby as she tried to smooth out the sign.

Missy and her parents anxiously scanned the faces of the people leaving the plane. Finally only a few passengers were left.

"You don't think she missed the plane, do you?" Missy asked.

"No, Jessica would have called us," said Mr. Fremont.

Just then, someone wearing sunglasses and a large purple broad-brimmed hat tapped Missy on the shoulder.

"I think you're looking for me," she said.

Missy stared at the girl, who took off her glasses. Missy could see that she was wearing a lot of make-up, including three different shades of purple eye shadow and bright red rouge on her cheeks. Missy wasn't even allowed to wear lipstick.

"Are you Tanya?" exclaimed Missy.

Tanya eyed Baby suspiciously. "Who did you expect, a dog walker?" she said sarcastically.

Mrs. Fremont stepped forward and gave Tanya a hug. "It's so good finally to meet you," said Mrs. Fremont. "I'm glad Missy put the sign on Baby to welcome you. We might have missed you completely. We weren't expecting some-one . . ." Mrs. Fremont paused. She really didn't know what to say. She wanted to say that they hadn't expected to see someone Missy's age who looked twice as old.

Mr. Fremont cleared his throat. "What your aunt Pat means is that we weren't expecting someone so tall," he said. "You're tall for your age."

Missy looked down at Tanya's feet. She was wearing silver high-top sneakers that had three-inch platform heels, but even without the heels she was a good three inches taller than Missy.

"I take ballet," said Tanya. "It's taught me good posture."

Missy tried to pull her shoulders back but forgot she was holding on to Baby's leash, and

she jerked his collar. Baby jumped up, bumping into Tanya.

Tanya stepped back. "Get him away from me!" she exclaimed.

"He's just trying to be friendly," said Missy.

"He probably sheds," complained Tanya, brushing off her spotless black stretch pants.

Missy hated to think what Baby could do to those pants if he *really* got friendly. The fact was that no matter how often Missy brushed Baby, he still shed—in clumps.

"Come on," said Mr. Fremont. "Let's get your luggage."

"I don't have any," said Tanya. "I like to travel light." She pointed to her knapsack.

"That's all you brought!" said Mr. Fremont admiringly. He was always complaining that Missy tried to bring her entire wardrobe on every trip.

Tanya nodded.

"Maybe you can give Missy some lessons on how to pack," said Mr. Fremont.

"Oh, great," mumbled Missy.

Missy, Baby, and Mrs. Fremont settled themselves in the back seat of the car. Tanya sat in the front because she said she got carsick. Missy suspected that it was because she didn't like Baby.

"How do we get out of here?" Mr. Fremont asked Missy as he looked at the maze of signs leading out of the airport. Mr. Fremont smiled at Tanya. "Missy's got an amazing sense of direction."

Missy pointed to the exit. "You go left, then take a right at the gas station," she said. Missy was proud of the fact that she had a good sense of direction.

"I've never understood why some people have a sense of direction and some don't," Mr. Fremont continued. "I read somewhere that it's memory. Just like musical pitch. I can remember what something should sound like, but I can never remember where I've just been."

"I never get lost," bragged Tanya. "And I can keep a tune. My singing teacher says I have *perfect* musical pitch."

Mr. Fremont laughed nervously. Missy looked out of the window and scowled. She couldn't keep a tune very well, but that never stopped her from singing.

When they got to the Fremonts' house, Missy was the first one to the front door. She opened the door with her key.

"We'll have to get a key made for Tanya," said Mr. Fremont. "Maybe that's the first thing you girls can do together."

"Great," said Missy flatly.

Her father picked up on her tone of voice. "Is anything wrong?" he whispered.

Missy shook her head. How could she tell her father that she was sure Tanya's visit was going to be a disaster?

"Come on, Tanya," sighed Missy. "I'll show you our room."

"We have to share a room?" Tanya asked.

"Tanya," said Missy's mother, "in this house it's share and share alike. Missy even cleaned up her room for you. She's worked hard to make you feel at home, right down to Baby's welcome sign."

Missy groaned to herself. She knew her mother was trying to be helpful, but the last thing she needed was for Tanya to feel guilty.

"It's okay, Mom," said Missy. "Tanya's probably been met by an Old English sheepdog carrying a WELCOME, COUSIN TANYA sign before, right?" Missy figured maybe she could ease things up with a joke.

Tanya stared at her. "Is that supposed to be funny?" she asked.

Missy rolled her eyes. Of all the put-downs, "Is that supposed to be funny?" had to be the worst! What was she going to do with a cousin who had no sense of humor!

"See what I mean?" Missy muttered to Baby as they followed Tanya up the stairs. "A total disaster!"

CHAPTER

3

Tanya snapped her fingers and swayed to the beat of the music coming through her headphones. Her side of the bedroom was perfectly neat. Missy's side wasn't quite as neat, but it wasn't a total mess either. To Missy's eyes, it looked more normal than Tanya's side.

Missy tapped Tanya on the arm. She had promised to show her the neighborhood.

"What would you like to see?" Missy shouted. "We can walk to the library. I can get you a temporary library card. I already asked the librarian, Mr. Vickers."

Tanya took her headphones off and hung them around her neck.

"Isn't there a mall around here? I thought kids like you always hung out in malls."

Missy shook her head. "Where did you get that idea? The mall's about six miles from here."

"I saw it on TV," said Tanya. "They showed all these bored kids hanging out in malls and getting into gang fights."

Missy looked out the window at the quiet block where they lived. "Uh, we don't have any gangs around here that I know about."

"So what *do* you do?"

"Well, we've got the library," Missy told her. "And we've got the community center. We can swim there or play basketball. And then, in a couple of weeks, we're both going to camp. Mom's already arranged it. This is my first time at this camp, and the director says we're both old enough to go on the compass scavenger hunt. They send you out into the wilds with nothing but a compass. It'll be neat."

Tanya laughed. "I can't believe people here really say *neat.*"

"What's wrong with saying *neat*?" asked Missy angrily.

"Did I say anything to annoy you?" Tanya asked innocently.

Missy didn't answer her. So far, just about everything Tanya said seemed to annoy Missy. And Tanya really seemed to enjoy making fun of Missy.

But Tanya was Missy's guest, and Missy was responsible for her.

"I'll tell you what," said Missy. "Why don't we go to the library and get you a card? Then we can go to the community center."

"I'm not used to so much excitement in one day," muttered Tanya.

"Look," snapped Missy. "If you're so bored already, why did you come here?"

"I didn't have much choice," said Tanya. She turned away from Missy. "Mom's in Europe, and it wasn't convenient for Dad to take me this summer. He's living in a one-room apartment."

"I'm sorry," said Missy. "Look, Indianapolis isn't so bad. You'll like it here." Missy felt guilty. She had forgotten why Tanya had come. Missy promised herself she would make sure that Tanya would have a good time.

"Let's go," said Missy. "Get your bathing suit."

Tanya looked a little embarrassed. "I didn't bring a bathing suit. I thought that because you're so far from the ocean . . . and I didn't think you'd have a pool."

"No problem," said Missy kindly. "You can borrow one of mine, and later, Mom will take us to the mall so you can buy a suit."

Missy took out her three bathing suits and showed them to Tanya. They were all one-piece racing suits. Missy's all-time favorite was a Wonder Woman suit, but she decided not to say a word if Tanya picked it.

"You don't care which one I take?" Tanya asked.

Missy shook her head.

"Hey, this Wonder Woman suit is so old-fashioned, it's almost an antique," Tanya said. "Really funky. I wouldn't have expected it of you."

Missy wasn't exactly sure she liked Tanya calling her favorite bathing suit old-fashioned, but

she was glad that Tanya thought it was "funky." She handed it to Tanya. "You can borrow it."

"Thanks," said Tanya. "It's a riot."

Tanya tried on the suit. Even though she was taller than Missy, it fit, and Missy had to admit it looked completely different on Tanya.

Tanya put on an extra-long man's shirt and belted it at her waist, so that she looked as if she were wearing a dress. Missy thought Tanya looked terrific, and she reminded herself to wear a shirt like that over her Wonder Woman bathing suit the next time.

They went downstairs. Mr. Fremont was on his way down to the basement to practice his viola. He stopped and looked at Tanya and Missy. "You girls look great," he said, smiling.

"Thanks, Uncle William," said Tanya. "I'm looking forward to going to the community center. It sounds like fun." Missy stared at her. Tanya certainly hadn't acted as if she thought it would be much fun a minute ago.

At the library Mr. Vickers greeted Missy with a big smile. "We got in some new mysteries," he said. Both Missy and Mr. Vickers loved mysteries.

"I like romances," said Tanya. "Don't they have any romances in this library?"

"Right over there," pointed Missy. She went over to the mystery section. Tanya picked out five romance paperbacks.

"I read fast," Tanya said.

"So do I," replied Missy, holding up the five books she had chosen.

They went to take out their books. Mr. Vickers helped Tanya fill out her form for a temporary library card. "I'm afraid that I can let you take out only two books until your card is processed," Mr. Vickers told Tanya. Just then a group of eight preschoolers came in. "Whoops, it's time for story hour," said Mr. Vickers. "I promised I'd dress up as a mouse for this afternoon's story. I've got to get my ears. Excuse me." He called to his assistant to check out Missy's and Tanya's books.

"He's weird," said Tanya.

"*I* think he's terrific," said Missy. "Sometimes I help him out with story hour. It's fun."

"You'd look cute in mouse ears," said Tanya. She looked down at the pile of books in her hand. "It's not fair," she pouted. "I can finish two books in a day. Why don't you take out the extra ones for me? You're allowed to take out as many as you want, aren't you?" She shoved her extra books at Missy. "Let's hurry! We're missing all the good rays for a suntan."

Missy sighed. She tended to burn instead of tan anyhow, but she took Tanya's books and checked them out on her card. Tanya was, after all, her guest.

The community center had an Olympic-sized pool, and Missy hoped that Tanya would be impressed. But Tanya looked as if something were missing.

"Don't you have a whirlpool?" she asked when they went into the locker room to change.

"Huh?" said Missy.

"At my mom's health club on the fifty-fifth floor of her office building, they have a whirlpool."

"Um . . . we don't have a whirlpool," admitted Missy. "We have whippoorwills and we have pussy willows, but no whirlpools. Hey, that could be a jingle for Indianapolis." She started to sing,

> Yes, we have no whirlpools,
> But whippoorwills . . . in Indianapolis . . .
> The city with no frills . . .
> That's where the fun is . . .

Tanya groaned. "Oh, no, there's this jerk at my school who keeps coming up with jingles for my mom. Don't *you* start."

"Missy Fremont, what in the world are you singing about?" asked a voice from the locker next door.

Missy groaned to herself. It was just her luck that Stephanie Cook would overhear her while Tanya was putting her down. Stephanie was Missy's classmate and neighbor. She was blond and pretty, and the best-dressed girl in Missy's class. She was also the most stuck-up. Missy and Stephanie were definitely *not* best friends, but over the past year, they had learned how to get along a little better.

Stephanie stepped out from her locker, wearing a bikini with a matching jacket.

"Hi, Stephanie," said Missy. "I want you to meet my cousin, Tanya Rosoff."

Stephanie looked up at Tanya. Almost everyone had to look up at Tanya, Missy realized. They walked out to the pool, where Tanya spread out her towel on the only available beach chair. Missy and Stephanie had to lie down on the concrete.

"I didn't know you had an older cousin," Stephanie said to Missy.

"We're the same age," said Missy. "Tanya's from New York."

"Neat," replied Stephanie.

In spite of herself, Missy giggled, and Tanya actually winked at her.

Stephanie looked confused.

"Sorry," said Tanya airily. "Just a joke between cousins."

"Did you two grow up together?" Stephanie asked.

"Actually, we'd never met until today," said Missy, giggling again.

"So?" asked Stephanie. "How long are you staying in Indianapolis?"

"Three weeks," answered Missy. "But for one of those weeks, she's coming to camp with us."

"Oh, then we'll be seeing a lot of each other." Stephanie smiled.

"I suppose so," said Tanya in a bored voice.

Missy couldn't believe it. Tanya was even more stuck-up than Stephanie was. She made Missy begin to feel a little sorry for Stephanie.

"Camp will be a lot of fun," said Stephanie. "This year we get to go on the compass scavenger hunt."

"I've heard," said Tanya. "A thrill, I'm sure."

"I guess you don't get to spend much time in the wilderness, coming from a big city like New York," said Stephanie.

"You don't know Central Park," said Tanya.

"I've always wanted to visit New York," Stephanie went on.

"It's *neat*," said Tanya sarcastically.

"Tanya's mom writes TV jingles," said Missy, glad for a reason to show off. "She wrote the Doggie Yum-Yums jingle—you know, the one with the dog that looks just like Baby. I was hoping my aunt could get Baby an audition."

Tanya lay back with her sunglasses hiding her eyes. "No way," she said. "They use only trained dogs."

"Baby's very well trained."

"You'd better not say anything against Missy's big Baby," said Stephanie. "She and that dog are inseparable."

"We'll see about that," said Tanya.

Missy wished she could see Tanya's eyes. Why had that sounded like a threat?

"I think I'll go in for a swim," said Missy.

"I'll go with you," said Stephanie. "How about you, Tanya?"

"No, thanks," replied Tanya. "It's not hot enough for me."

Since the temperature was over eighty-five, Missy wondered what Tanya would consider hot enough.

Missy and Stephanie dove into the cool water. They started to swim laps side by side.

"Your cousin's a little weird, isn't she?" Stephanie said.

"She's not weird," said Missy. "She's sophisticated."

But Missy felt very confused. If you asked
her, there didn't seem to be much of a differ-
ence between sophisticated and weird.

CHAPTER

4

———

Missy and Tanya were alone in the house. Mr. Fremont had a concert, and Mrs. Fremont had a front-row seat. Missy had looked forward to this evening—they'd have the whole place to themselves.

"Don't worry about us," Missy had said as her parents left. "We have Baby as a watchdog."

Mrs. Fremont had laughed. "Baby has many great virtues, but I wouldn't say that being a fierce watchdog was among them."

"He'd probably wag his stump of a tail at a burglar and show him where you keep the silver," Tanya said. "But we'll be okay, Aunt Pat. You have fun."

Mrs. Fremont had looked at Mr. Fremont. "It sounds to me like these two have big plans."

"Oh, yeah," Tanya had joked. "We're going to do all kinds of neat stuff."

At first Missy had been excited by the idea of

being in the house alone, but it turned out to be a pretty boring evening. Tanya took a long bubble bath while Missy watched some TV by herself. Then Tanya said she was tired and wanted to go to sleep.

They both got ready for bed. Baby lay down at the foot of Missy's bed the way he always did.

"Did you know that your dog snores in the night?" asked Tanya.

"He does not," said Missy, blushing. Missy always blushed when she lied. Actually she had to admit that Baby did make some pretty weird noises when he slept. "I wouldn't exactly call it snoring."

"I'd call it disgusting," said Tanya. "And I've heard it every night for a week now. It keeps me up."

"Oh," said Missy. "Is that why you sleep so late?" Missy was getting sick of not being able to use her room in the morning.

"I've got to sleep *some*time," insisted Tanya.

"I thought you slept in the bathtub," said Missy. It seemed to her that Tanya spent hours in the bathroom.

"I like a hot bath," Tanya said casually.

"I know," retorted Missy. "That's why there's never any hot water left for me."

Baby got up and padded in between the two beds. Baby never liked it when people argued. His head moved from left to right as he looked at the two girls. Then he sat down and lifted his front paws.

"What's he doing?" demanded Tanya, pulling the covers up to her chin.

Missy giggled. "He's trying to get us to make up."

"He's stupid if he thinks he can do that," said Tanya.

"Stop calling him stupid all the time. I think he's sweet. Baby hates it whenever anyone gets angry. The few times that Mom and Dad fight, he actually whimpers."

"He would have loved it at our house," muttered Tanya.

Baby put his paws up on Tanya's bed.

"Get him away from me!" cried Tanya. "I don't want that dumb dog on my bed."

"Come on, Baby," said Missy, turning off her light. "Come over here where you're wanted."

Missy fell into a sound sleep. Suddenly, she woke up with a start. Someone was shaking her, hard. Missy opened her eyes and saw Tanya standing by her bed.

"Missy, wake up!" Tanya whispered hoarsely. "Wake up!"

Missy shook herself awake.

"What time is it?" Missy yawned.

"Eleven-thirty," answered Tanya.

"In the morning?" exclaimed Missy.

"No, at night," whispered Tanya. "Keep your voice down."

"Why?" whispered Missy.

"There's someone downstairs," whispered Tanya. "I think it's a burglar."

Missy listened. She couldn't hear anything. The house seemed quiet . . . too quiet, in fact. Their room was *much* too quiet.

"Baby . . . Here, Baby," Missy whispered.

There wasn't the shuffling noise Baby usually made as he padded to the bed.

"Where is he?" exclaimed Missy, turning on the light. The room was empty.

"Shhh." Tanya turned off the light. "You don't want the burglar to know we're up here, do you?"

"Do you think he's got Baby?" Missy asked.

"Who cares about Baby?" Tanya demanded.

"I do," insisted Missy. "I've got to go down there and rescue him." She threw back the covers.

"Forget about him," Tanya said. "We've got to save ourselves!"

"Baby must have gone downstairs to investigate," said Missy.

"I wish you'd stop worrying about him," said Tanya. "Worry about me, instead. My poor parents sent me all the way to Indianapolis, where they thought I'd be safe!"

"You'd better stay here," said Missy. She got out of bed and tiptoed to her closet. She opened the door carefully, worried that the burglar might hear it squeak. She hesitated, listening with all her might for sounds of the burglar.

Then she heard a faint scratching noise. It came from somewhere downstairs.

Missy wanted to jump back into bed and pull the covers over her head. "You're right," she whispered. "I hear something downstairs too."

"It sounds like a motor, right?" said Tanya. "That must be his safecracking equipment."

"We don't have a safe," said Missy. "It sounded like something scratching. Maybe they've tied up Baby."

"No, it sounds scarier than that," insisted Tanya.

"What could be scarier than a creep who would tie up a poor defenseless dog?" whispered Missy. She reached into the closet and got out her baseball bat.

Then she opened the bedroom door.

"Where are you going?" hissed Tanya.

"To rescue Baby. You stay here."

"You're not leaving me alone," said Tanya, getting out of bed. She cowered behind Missy as they started down the stairs.

Missy strained her ears. The scratching noise was growing louder.

Suddenly Tanya grabbed her arm so tightly, Missy almost jumped into the air.

"There it is," whispered Tanya. "Do you hear it?"

Missy looked in the direction Tanya was pointing—toward the kitchen. "What are you talking about?" Missy asked.

"The noise," whispered Tanya. "Can't you hear it?"

Missy cocked her head. "All I hear is the refrigerator. It's making ice."

Tanya let go of Missy's arm. "The refrigerator?"

Missy tiptoed into the kitchen, waving the baseball bat in front of her. The kitchen was empty and the refrigerator was quiet. Then it made a whirring sound as the motor turned on.

"That's it," said Tanya, looking a little embarrassed. "That's the noise I heard."

"You thought the refrigerator was a burglar!" exclaimed Missy.

"Well, it's so quiet here, every noise sounds loud. In New York it's never quiet. I got scared."

Missy stared at her. "Of a refrigerator?"

Tanya shrugged. "Okay, so I was wrong. Big deal. Let's go back upstairs."

"Baby," said Missy. "We still haven't found Baby."

"I want to go back to bed," said Tanya, wrapping her arms around herself. "It's creepy down here alone."

"We're not going anywhere until we find Baby," insisted Missy.

"Look, he's a dog," said Tanya. "Aren't dogs supposed to wander around at night?"

"Not Baby. He sleeps at the foot of my bed all night. He always has, ever since he was a little puppy."

"How touching," said Tanya, rolling her eyes.

Missy cocked her head. She heard a slight scratching noise. "What's that?"

"It's probably the toaster," said Tanya sarcastically.

"Shhh," said Missy. She heard the noise again. "It's coming from the basement."

Tanya grabbed Missy's arm. "I don't want to go down there," she said.

Missy picked up the baseball bat again. "We have to go. Baby may be in trouble."

Missy's heart was beating extra fast as she walked down the backstairs to the basement. She put her ear to the closed door.

"Baby," Missy whispered.

She heard a low woof from the other side of the door.

Missy tried to open the door. It wouldn't budge. She looked up. The basement door had a top lock that the Fremonts never used. But now the lock was bolted tight. Missy tried to reach the lock, but she couldn't.

"Tanya, can you help me?"

No one answered. Missy turned around. Tanya was nowhere to be seen.

"Hold on, Baby," urged Missy. Missy got the stepladder and slid back the bolt.

Baby bounded out the door, practically knocking Missy over in his excitement. His coat was covered with dust from the basement.

Baby licked Missy's face. Missy hugged him. "It's okay, Baby," she crooned to him. "It's okay. But how did you get in there?"

Missy's eyes traveled upstairs. "Tanya," Missy muttered.

She ran up the stairs two at a time. Baby raced ahead of her, bounding up the steps four at a time.

Baby slid to a stop in front of Missy's bedroom. The bedroom door was shut tight.

Missy opened it.

Tanya was in bed with her face to the wall, breathing deeply.

Missy jumped on Tanya's bed. "Why did you do it?" shouted Missy.

"Do what?" Tanya asked, rubbing her eyes.

"Stop pretending. You weren't asleep just now," Missy said angrily. "You locked Baby up in the basement. Why did you do such a creepy thing?"

"I didn't do anything," retorted Tanya. "I can't

help it if your dumb dog got stuck in the basement."

"Give me a break! I suppose *he* bolted the top lock from the outside. Just call him Wonder Dog."

Tanya smiled and turned her back on Missy. "The lock's open now, isn't it?" asked Tanya.

"Sure," replied Missy in a puzzled voice. "I had to unlock it to get Baby out."

"Then you can't prove it was ever locked," Tanya said sweetly. "He could have gotten stuck all by himself."

Missy stared at her. Tanya was right. There was no way she could prove that Tanya had locked up Baby.

But why had she done it?

There could be only one explanation.

"You're just plain mean," muttered Missy.

But Tanya had pulled the covers up over her ears and pretended to be fast asleep.

CHAPTER

5

Missy looked longingly at her Wonder Woman bathing suit lying on the edge of Tanya's bed. Tanya lay on top of her bed reading one of the books she had taken out on Missy's library card. Missy looked at the card in the front of her book and realized the books were due that day.

Missy wished she could put a card in her bathing suit to remind Tanya about giving it back. Tanya had been wearing the suit every day, and so far she'd made no move to go out and buy her own. Missy knew she should have the nerve to bring up the subject, but Tanya seemed to consider the bathing suit hers now.

Missy went downstairs. In the kitchen her father was making spaghetti sauce.

"Do you need any help?" Missy asked him.

"You're on cleanup duty," said Mr. Fremont. "Your mother and I are going out to dinner tonight. This is for you and Tanya, and I'll freeze the rest."

Missy took a spoon and tasted the spaghetti sauce.

"What's wrong?" asked her father.

"Oh, nothing," sighed Missy. She had hardly tasted the sauce. Just the idea of eating dinner alone with Tanya made her heart sink.

"I expect more enthusiasm from my best eater," said Mr. Fremont.

"Sorry, Dad. It's delicious," said Missy in a flat voice.

Mr. Fremont tasted his sauce. "Maybe it needs more oregano." He glanced at Missy. "How are you and Tanya getting along?"

Missy sighed again. She couldn't tell her father that Tanya was turning out to be a terrible guest. After all, inviting Tanya had been her idea. Missy knew that her parents wanted Tanya to have a good time.

"You know, nobody expected you to be instant friends," said her father shrewdly. "You two have got to give each other a chance."

"I'm giving her lots of chances," said Missy, thinking of her swimsuit that seemed to have become Tanya's private property.

Mr. Fremont put a large handful of spaghetti into a pot of boiling water. "I think you're pretty terrific," he said. "It's not every girl who would invite a perfect stranger into her home, even if the stranger is her cousin."

"Cousins can be pretty strange," said Missy.

Mr. Fremont laughed. "Well, I like the way you've tried to make her feel at home."

Just then Mrs. Fremont came into the kitchen. "What a mess," she moaned. "Honey, we're going to be late."

"Don't worry, Mom," said Missy, suddenly feeling very good about her parents. "I'll clean it all up."

"Thanks," said Mrs. Fremont. "I have an exam tomorrow, and when I get back, I really have to study." Mrs. Fremont, a kindergarten teacher, was taking a summer school course in science.

"Mom, I promise," said Missy. "I'll clean up. It's my turn, anyway."

After her parents left, Missy finished making dinner and called Tanya.

After ten minutes of waiting for Tanya to come down to dinner, Missy finally went upstairs to get her. "Didn't you hear me call you?" said Missy. "Dinner's ready. It's just you and me tonight."

Tanya didn't look up from her book.

"You know our books were due back at the library today," Missy said in an annoyed voice.

"I'll be finished with this one in a minute, and then you can take it back. Is the library open tonight?"

Missy looked up at the library schedule on her bulletin board. "It's open till eight-thirty tonight, and then it will be closed for the weekend. But it's my turn to do the dishes after dinner. I promised Mom. I'll never have time to get to the library."

Tanya quickly scanned the last page of her book. Then she tossed it on Missy's bed. "So, why don't you take the books back, and I'll do the dishes for you."

"You did them last night," said Missy. "Are you sure you don't mind?"

"No problem," said Tanya. She handed Missy a plastic bag. "The rest of my books are in this bag."

Missy took the bag and stuffed her mystery books inside.

"Thanks," she said. "I really appreciate this. Do you want me to take out some more books for you?"

Tanya nodded. "Yeah, you know the kind of books I like."

"Right," said Missy. "I'll just look for the books that I wouldn't want."

"So we've got opposite tastes," said Tanya. "That's not so bad, is it?"

"I guess you're right," said Missy. "Sorry."

Missy just couldn't decide about Tanya. Sometimes she was nice, but most of the time she acted as if Missy and all of Indianapolis were a huge pain in the neck.

After dinner Missy looked at the messy pots, pans, and dishes in the kitchen. "Are you *sure* you don't mind cleaning up?" she asked Tanya.

"I *said* I'd do the dishes. You'd better get going."

"Are you *sure* you don't mind being in the house by yourself?" Missy asked. She felt a little guilty about leaving Tanya alone with all those dirty dishes.

"Don't be ridiculous," said Tanya impatiently. "I'll leave Baby with you to keep you company," said Missy. Baby put his head down between his paws as if he didn't feel too happy about that idea.

"I do *not* need a watchdog," Tanya snapped. "Take him with you."

"I can't," said Missy. "I'm not allowed to take Baby out at night unless he's wearing his special collar. It reflects headlights so he won't get hit."

"I'd feel sorry for the car that hit *him*!" Tanya muttered.

"Well, anyway, his collar's broken, so I can't take him with me."

Tanya gave Baby a dirty look. "All right, he can stay. Just stop making such a big deal about it. If you have to go, go."

"Okay, I'm *going*," said Missy in an exasperated voice. She couldn't believe that just a little while ago she was beginning to think that she and her cousin were becoming friends.

Baby picked his head up when Missy put on her jacket. Missy patted him on the head. "Stay, boy," she said.

Baby whined. He hated the words *Stay, boy*.

"You'll be okay, Baby," whispered Missy. "Just keep out of Terrible Tanya's way."

"What's that?" demanded Tanya.

"Nothing," said Missy. "I was just telling Baby to be good and to mind you."

Tanya looked at Missy suspiciously.

Baby gave Tanya a sideways glance and then padded off to his bed, a sort of nest that Missy had made for him out of old towels.

"I'll be back soon," promised Missy.

"Don't hurry on my account," said Tanya.

Missy rolled her eyes. Why did Tanya have to go out of her way to be such a pain? Missy felt sorry for Baby, leaving him alone with her.

But she put the bag of books in her bike basket and took off for the library, leaving Baby behind.

Mr. Vickers was at the return desk in the children's room. "Hi, Missy, I was hoping you'd stop by today. I wondered if you wanted to volunteer for a story hour or two this summer."

"Gee, I'd love to," answered Missy. "But I'll be going to camp next week."

"How about doing it before you go? I could really use your help this week. And I thought you'd be great acting out *Dracula Is a Pain in the Neck*."

Missy giggled. "That sounds like fun. I'll bring my cousin Tanya along. She's visiting from New York." Missy paused, then asked, "Is there a part for a dog in it? I could bring Baby along too. Baby's great with little kids."

"Sure, bring him along," said Mr. Vickers. "I'd be glad for the help. I've got a group of fifteen preschoolers coming in on Tuesday, and I sure could use someone I can trust to keep them in line."

"I'll be there," said Missy, proud that Mr. Vickers had asked her and proud that he trusted her.

Missy put the bag of books down on the desk. "These are due today," she said.

Mr. Vickers pulled out the books. He held one up and frowned. The book's cover was all wrinkled and the pages were swollen to twice their normal size. It was obvious that the book had fallen into some water.

Missy stared at the book, horrified.

"What happened to this?" Mr. Vickers asked in a stern voice.

"I don't know," Missy gasped.

"What do you mean, you don't know? You took it out."

"Yes . . . I did . . ." stammered Missy. "But I didn't know it was going to look like that. You see, my cousin took it out . . . but she took it out on my card. Remember, she had to get a temporary card, and . . ."

Missy stopped chattering and watched in horror as Mr. Vickers pulled out the other books. Missy couldn't believe it. Every one of the books Tanya had taken out looked like they had been dropped into the bathtub.

"So that's what Tanya does when she takes those long baths," Missy muttered to herself.

"Missy," said Mr. Vickers. "I'm afraid these books are ruined. If they were taken out on your card, you're responsible for their condition."

"I know," wailed Missy. "But I didn't do it. Look, Mr. Vickers, these aren't even the kind of books I like. You know I read only mysteries. These are yucky romances."

"That's not the point," said Mr. Vickers sternly. "You shouldn't have let anyone else use your card. That's a rule in this library, and you should know that!"

"It wasn't just 'anyone else,'" said Missy. "It was my cousin."

Mr. Vickers piled up the ruined books on his desk. There were five of them. "I'm just surprised that you didn't mention it to me earlier," he said.

"I didn't know about it until now," said Missy. "Do you still want me to help out on Tuesday?"

Mr. Vickers sighed. "Yes, of course." But he sounded cool, as if he were no longer quite sure.

"What do I do about the books?" Missy asked.

"I'm afraid you'll have to pay for them," Mr. Vickers replied. "I'll look up the cost of replacing the books, and we'll send you a bill."

Missy nodded. "I guess I can't take out any new books either."

"I think you should wait until you clear up your account," said Mr. Vickers.

"Great," mumbled Missy. "Now I have nothing new to read tonight."

"I'm sorry, Missy," said Mr. Vickers. "But there are rules."

"Don't I know it," said Missy.

Missy got on her bicycle. "Tanya Rosoff," she said to herself, as she pedaled furiously for home, "it's time *you* learned the rules. You're going to pay for those books—or else!"

CHAPTER

6

Missy slammed the front door. She barreled into the kitchen, practically knocking over Baby. She didn't hear his warning bark until it was too late.

Missy's mother stood by the sink, her arms folded.

Pots and pans were piled high in the kitchen sink. Not one pot had been washed. The dishes that Missy and Tanya had eaten from weren't even cleared from the table.

"Where were you?" demanded Mrs. Fremont.

"Uh . . . at the library," said Missy.

"How nice for you," said Mrs. Fremont. "And what do you call this kitchen?"

"A mess?" said Missy weakly.

"I'd say that's an understatement," said Mrs. Fremont. "What happened to your promise? I explained to you that I had to study tonight. Where am I supposed to put my books?" Mrs.

Fremont pointed to the kitchen table, where she usually did her studying.

"Tanya!" screamed Missy.

"This is between you and me," said Mrs. Fremont. "There is no reason to bring Tanya into it."

"But she promised to do the dishes while I returned our library books . . . and then the books she gave me were ruined. . . . TANYA!"

Missy raised her voice even louder and screamed, "*TANYA!*"

Mrs. Fremont put her hands over her ears.

Tanya came downstairs in her bathrobe, a towel wrapped around her head.

"What's all the screaming about? I was in the shower."

"Probably using my shampoo," muttered Missy.

"What is your problem?" Tanya demanded. "I have to put conditioner on; otherwise my hair will be all tangled."

"Look at the kitchen!" Missy yelled. "You promised!"

"Promised what?" asked Tanya, looking innocently at Mrs. Fremont.

"Somebody is in trouble here," said Mrs. Fremont. "I thought we had a cleanup system worked out for the summer."

Missy looked at Tanya. "You promised to do the dishes tonight," said Missy, trying hard not to scream.

Tanya didn't look at Missy. "It was your turn to do them, right?"

"Is that true, Missy?" Mrs. Fremont asked,

walking over to the refrigerator where the schedule was held up by a magnet.

"If you look at the schedule, it's true," said Missy. "But Tanya said she'd do them. She's lying."

"I wouldn't call me a liar if I were you," warned Tanya.

"That's what you are!" yelled Missy. "You're a liar . . . and . . . a book abuser!"

Tanya looked at Mrs. Fremont and rolled her eyes as if they were both adults and Missy were the only child in the room.

"Aunt Pat, I simply do not know what she is talking about," Tanya said.

"Do you deny that you said you'd do the dishes?" asked Missy.

"Are you studying to be a lawyer?" asked Tanya.

"*Answer my question!*" screamed Missy.

"Missy," said her mother. "Lower your voice. It was your turn to do the dishes. It's your responsibility to see that they get done. I don't care who said what."

"Excuse me," said Tanya. "I really must get that conditioner on my hair."

Mrs. Fremont turned to Missy, who was almost in tears. "I'm going out for a walk," said Mrs. Fremont, taking Baby's leash. "I expect to see this kitchen cleaned up and you cooled down by the time I get back."

"But . . . Mom . . ." stammered Missy.

"I don't want to hear another word," said Mrs. Fremont. Baby gave Missy a backward glance as he went out the door with Mrs. Fremont. Missy knew her mother was angry. But it wasn't fair! How could Tanya tell such a bold-faced lie? Missy couldn't believe it.

She raced up the stairs and into the bathroom. Tanya stepped out of the shower daintily.

"How could you lie?" Missy yelled.

Tanya looked at her, her eyes wide. "I didn't want to get in trouble."

"But you got me in trouble! How could you?"

"You live here!"

"What's that got to do with it?" Missy felt like strangling Tanya.

Tanya shrugged.

"And not only did you lie to my mother," yelled Missy, "you gave me books to return to the library that you dumped in the bathtub!"

"But you can't prove it," Tanya said sweetly. "I'll say I gave them back to you in good condition."

"You don't make any bones about lying," said Missy in a shocked voice.

"Adults always believe me," said Tanya. "And your parents are pushovers."

"They are not," protested Missy. "Mom and Dad can be plenty tough."

Tanya laughed, but it wasn't a nice laugh. "You don't know what tough is."

"I do too."

"Yeah, you sure are some tough cookie. Admit it. Your parents are soft on you . . . maybe it's because you were adopted."

Missy could hardly breathe.

"How did you know that?" she gasped.

"It's no secret, is it?" said Tanya matter-of-factly. "My mom told me you were adopted when we got your invitation."

"No, of course it's not a secret," said Missy. "I was just surprised that you knew. And that you'd think it's a good reason for my parents to be 'soft on me.' Anyway," Missy added, "my parents aren't soft on me. Didn't you see how angry Mom was?"

"You call *that* angry? That was nothing! Let's face it, Missy, your parents treat you like a china doll. You and your dumb dog. *Baaaaby.*" Tanya drew out the name, laughing at Missy.

"Don't you call my dog dumb. You don't deserve to call him anything."

"Wow," said Tanya sarcastically. "I've never seen someone protect the honor of a dog before."

"You don't know the first thing about honor," Missy retorted. She slammed the door to the bathroom and went downstairs, where she furiously scraped out the pots and pans.

Just as she was finishing, Mrs. Fremont walked back inside. Baby was panting and padded right over to his water dish.

"I think I walked a little too fast for Baby," said Mrs. Fremont, sitting down at the clean kitchen table. "How are you doing?"

"As you can see, the kitchen is clean," Missy snapped.

"That's not what I meant," said Mrs. Fremont gently. "I'm sorry I yelled at you. Now, tell me, just what was going on here?"

"I don't want to talk about it," mumbled Missy.

"I think we have to," said Mrs. Fremont.

"There's nothing to talk about. You believed Tanya, not me. Everyone thinks she's so terrific, so tall, so sophisticated. Tanya would never do anything wrong."

"Where is she?" Mrs. Fremont asked.

"Upstairs," Missy muttered as she finished scouring the last pot.

"What's been going on between you two, anyway?" Mrs. Fremont asked.

"Hate at first sight?" Missy suggested.

Mrs. Fremont heaved a sigh. "Nobody ever said you had to love all your relatives, but we have to give Tanya a chance."

"She lied, Mom. Honest."

Mrs. Fremont nodded her head. "I believe you."

"You're not just being soft on me because I was adopted?" asked Missy.

Mrs. Fremont looked shocked. "Did Tanya say that?"

"Yes."

To Missy's surprise, her mother laughed. "Do you think we're soft on you?"

Missy thought of all the schedules and work that she did around the house. "Not exactly."

"We love you, Missy. Tanya doesn't know anything about how we live our lives," said Mrs. Fremont. "She's trying to fit in, and I think she's having a hard time."

"The only place she'd fit would be at a bath-takers' convention," said Missy.

Her mother laughed again. Then she got serious. "Missy, I know it's difficult, but look at things from Tanya's point of view. She doesn't know anybody here, and she's going through a rough time at home. Promise me you'll give her another chance. I think this is one case where you have to go more than halfway. We all do."

Missy promised. But she wondered just how far she'd have to go.

CHAPTER 7

Tanya put on one of the black capes that Mrs. Fremont had made for them. She had even made a cape for Baby to wear at Mr. Vickers's story hour.

"This is too good to waste on a bunch of four-year-olds," said Tanya. "I think I'll take it to camp with me."

"Great, everyone will think you're a real vampire," said Missy. She put her hand over her mouth. What had happened to her promise to give Tanya another chance? Missy vowed not to let anything Tanya said bother her.

Tanya put on the fangs she and Missy had bought. "The better to eat you up, my dear," she said.

"Hey, stop kidding around."

"What makes you think I'm kidding," said Tanya, chomping her plastic fangs up and down.

"We've got to be careful not to scare the little kids too much," warned Missy. But she knew she was talking as much about herself as she was about the little kids.

Mr. Vickers was waiting for them at the library. "It's nice of you both to help out," said Mr. Vickers.

"Oh, I was glad to," said Tanya. "I love libraries, and I like to do all I can to help little kids learn to love books as much as I do."

Missy thought about the drowned books. She couldn't believe how Tanya could say one thing to her and then be completely different around adults.

Mr. Vickers looked at Tanya admiringly. "You've got a wonderful cousin, Missy. Maybe she can teach you a little respect for books."

"Missy told me about that accident she had," said Tanya. "She felt awful. I'm teaching her not to read in the bathtub, at least not library books."

"That's a lesson you should already have learned," said Mr. Vickers to Missy.

Missy didn't say anything. She was wondering how she was ever going to become friends with a two-faced liar like Tanya.

"Well, children," said Mr. Vickers as the little boys and girls sat in a circle around him. "We have a real treat for you today. Would you ever think we'd get three vampires at story hour?"

"*Ohhhhh,*" cried fifteen little voices as Missy wrapped the cape around herself and jumped into the middle of the circle, followed by Baby dressed in a black cape too.

"Have you ever seen a four-footed vampire?" Missy asked the group.

"I am the queen of the vampires," shouted

Tanya. Missy looked up, startled. That wasn't at all what they had planned. Tanya was supposed to come out and say, "I am a vampire, and have I got a story for you." Then she would take the book out of her cape and start to read it.

Tanya took center stage. She swept her cape in wide circles and covered Missy and Baby with it.

The kids all laughed.

Missy tried to get the cape off her, but it got tangled in Baby's leash. Soon Missy and Baby were both buried by Tanya's cape.

Tanya laughed wickedly. "I'm afraid we've lost two of our vampires, but since I am the queen, I will tell you a story."

Tanya sat down right on top of Missy and Baby. The kids laughed and laughed as Baby managed to peek his head out one end of Tanya's cape and Missy edged out of the other.

Tanya playfully bopped both of them on the head, but she got Missy with her knuckles and it hurt. Baby gave a little yelp. Missy was furious.

The kids laughed even harder. Missy noticed Mr. Vickers in the back, smiling happily.

"A queen, boys and girls, has to know how to make her subjects behave. Now, how do you think a queen of the vampires keeps order?" Tanya asked.

Several kids in the front row raised their hands. Tanya pointed to a little boy who was wearing a wrestling T-shirt.

"What would you do if you were king of the vampires?" she asked him.

"I'd bite everybody," said the boy.

"You'd make a good vampire," said Tanya approvingly. "But, as queen of the vampires, I am very busy. I don't get to fool around the way other vampires do. Why, just look at how my subjects are squirming around right now."

Tanya stood up. She swept her cape off Missy and Baby. Missy felt like a fool, lying on the floor on top of Baby.

She stood up and glared at Tanya.

"I'm afraid one of my subjects is angry," said Tanya. "I'll just have to show her who's boss."

Tanya chased Missy around the circle, trying to bite her. Missy ran away, and Baby chased Tanya, barking.

The kids laughed and clapped, and even Mr. Vickers applauded.

Tanya stopped and bowed as if it had all been planned. Missy stood next to her, not knowing exactly what to do. Tanya took her hand and pulled on it. Missy took a bow too.

"That was wonderful, girls," said Mr. Vickers, still clapping his hands. "Very original."

"A little too original," muttered Missy under her breath as they walked away.

"The kids loved it," said Tanya. "I thought it would be boring just to read a story."

"But you didn't tell me. You just made fun of me and Baby. If we had talked about it, we could have done something really funny."

"We did," said Tanya.

"*You* did," said Missy angrily. "You made me feel like a jerk."

"Takes one to know one," taunted Tanya in a singsong voice.

After Mr. Vickers returned the children to their parents, he came over to them. He was grinning from ear to ear. "I can't thank you enough, girls," he said. "I'm sorry I'm losing both of you to camp next week."

"I'd like to lose *you* at camp," Missy hissed at Tanya. Mr. Vickers didn't hear her.

"Tanya, I wish you lived in Indianapolis all year round," said Mr. Vickers. "Don't you, Missy?"

Missy's eyes opened wide. She wished Tanya lived here full-time almost as much as she wished that she lived with a family of vampires.

"I think Missy is so overcome with the thought that she's speechless," said Tanya. "Isn't that right, Missy?"

But Missy had picked up Baby's leash and was on her way out the door. "Tanya Rosoff, or Miss Dracula, I should say," she muttered as she led Baby down the steps of the library, "that was your last chance to be friends!"

CHAPTER

8

Missy and Tanya were in Missy's bedroom packing for camp. Baby padded into the room, sniffed at Missy's knapsack, and whimpered.

"It's okay, Baby," said Missy, bending down to give him a hug. "I won't be gone long. Only a week."

Missy stood up. "Excuse me," she said in an overly polite voice.

"Yes?" replied Tanya as she stuffed Missy's Wonder Woman bathing suit inside her knapsack.

"I wondered if you were through with my bathing suit."

Tanya raised her eyebrows. "No, I'm not," she said.

"It's *my* bathing suit," said Missy angrily. "And I want it back!"

"I'll give it back when I feel like it!" Tanya snapped.

Just then, Mr. Fremont poked his head into

the room. "Are you two ready for the drive to camp?" he asked.

"I am," said Tanya, hoisting her knapsack on her back. "Missy is still looking for her bathing suit." Tanya left the room.

"Better get a move on, honey," said Mr. Fremont. "Do you need help finding your bathing suit?"

"No," said Missy with a sigh. "I know just where it is."

Missy stuffed her old, worn-out striped bathing suit into her knapsack. "I'm ready," she said, picking up her sleeping bag.

When the Fremonts and Tanya arrived at camp, Missy's friends from school, Emily and Willie, came running up to her. "Hi, come on, we're in your tent. We saved you a bed." Tanya stood by Missy's side, pretending not to care that she didn't know anybody. Missy introduced Tanya to her friends.

"Let's go to our tent and get this over with," said Tanya. "My knapsack is heavy."

"Yeah, it's got half my stuff in it," muttered Missy. She saw her mother looking at her.

Missy gave her mother a hug. " 'Bye, Mom, you'd better go now. Camp rules say parents can only drop off their kids. Then they have to leave."

"I know," said Mrs. Fremont, giving Missy a big hug. "You have a wonderful time. I've got only one order, just have fun."

Missy kissed her. She knew her mom realized

that having Tanya as a house guest had not turned out to be a bed of roses.

Missy gave Baby a hug and a kiss. Baby licked her face. "Be good," Missy told him. "I'll see you soon."

Next, Missy went to hug her father. "Have fun," said Mr. Fremont.

"Mom already told me that. In fact, she made it an order."

"Well, it's an order from me too," said Mr. Fremont. "Try to help Tanya have a good time too," he whispered, giving her a squeeze.

Missy sighed. She didn't want to tell her father that both things were impossible. She couldn't possibly have a good time if she still had to worry about Tanya.

Missy kissed her father. "Come on, Tanya," she said. "Let's go see our tent. You'll like Emily and Willie. They're neat."

Tanya rolled her eyes. "There's that word again," she said. "When I get back to New York, it's going to take me weeks to learn to talk like a normal person."

Missy wanted to say that she thought Tanya would never be a normal person, but she held her tongue, thinking about her father.

Inside the tent Missy could see that she was going to have a problem. Stephanie had staked out one side of the tent as her territory. There were two empty beds beside her. The tent had three beds to a side. Missy could sleep with her friends, Emily and Willie, where they'd be able to giggle and whisper and have fun. Or she could sleep with Tanya and Stephanie.

Tanya looked at Missy. "Where are you going to sleep?"

"Uh . . . I don't know," stammered Missy, stalling for time.

"There's room for both of you over here." Stephanie pointed to the beds next to her.

Missy looked longingly at the bed next to Emily and Willie.

"Come on, Missy," said Tanya. "I guess we're going to be kissing cousins to the end."

"Um . . . I promised Emily and Willie I'd sleep next to them," said Missy. She put her knapsack on the bed.

Tanya looked hurt and Missy immediately felt bad, but not bad enough that she wanted to sleep next to Tanya. "What's the matter?" said Tanya to Emily. "Are you afraid of the dark?"

Emily stared at her. "Of course not. I just like Missy."

Tanya laughed nastily. "Isn't that sweet? I knew somebody had to."

"What's wrong with your cousin?" Willie whispered.

"Don't ask," Missy whispered back.

"Trading secrets. How cute!" said Tanya. "I'm going to look around. I can't believe I'm stuck here in the woods for a whole week."

"I'll go with you," offered Missy.

"I want to be alone," Tanya insisted.

"But you don't know the area," protested Missy. "You could get lost in the woods. Let me go with you. We can look for the lake."

"I don't need anyone," said Tanya. She pulled up the tent flap and ran out.

"Does she always act that way?" Emily asked.

Missy bit her lip. "She's not easy to get along with."

"Easy!" exclaimed Willie. "She acts like she wants to bite our heads off."

"Well, she does have certain vampire tendencies," said Missy, giggling. She told them about Tanya's vampire act at the library.

"She's probably high-strung," sniffed Stephanie. "I bet living in New York does that to you. Well, I certainly don't want to sleep next to *her.* I'm going to pick another bed."

Stephanie moved her things down one bed, so that the counselor would have to sleep between Tanya and her.

"Hey, you can't just make her sleep by herself," said Missy.

"She's *not* by herself," Stephanie replied. "She's next to the counselor."

Missy picked up her knapsack and sleeping bag.

"Where are you going?" asked Emily.

"I'm going to sleep next to my cousin," said Missy.

Emily helped her move. "This sure isn't the way I thought camp would be," she said.

"You're talking about my *whole summer*," said Missy.

Tanya came back a few minutes later. She saw that Missy had moved. "Don't tell me that you missed me so much, you had to sleep next to me."

"That's right," said Missy.

Just then, Susan, their counselor, opened the tent flap. She was a short young woman, about eighteen years old. She wore an Indiana U. sweat shirt and had a really nice smile. Missy knew she was going to like having Susan as a counselor.

"You must be Missy and Tanya," said Susan. "I think you two are our only new campers this year. We're glad to have you both. Have you ever been to camp before?"

Missy nodded. "I went to Girl Scout camp for a week last summer."

"Luckily, no," said Tanya. "I've never been to camp!"

"I hope Missy warned you about our wilderness survival course," Susan said to Tanya. "We have a compass scavenger hunt. We send you out in pairs, and you have to follow a route just by studying your compass. It's a lot of fun. This is the first year that your group of campers is old enough to do it."

"Aren't I the lucky one," said Tanya. "I've been hearing about this event since the day I arrived."

"I want to win it," insisted Missy. "I've finally found a contest where my great sense of direction will count."

"What do you get if you win?" asked Tanya.

"The glory," said Missy. "And a trophy."

"Oh, goody," said Tanya sarcastically.

Missy had only one hope—that she and Tanya would *not* be paired together.

"I hear it's really scary," said Willie. "You get to take only one canteen of water for the two of

you, and just a couple of candy bars. You can eat the edible berries. So you'd better pay attention to the nature course."

Tanya gave Willie her bored-to-death look. "Would you please tell me why I would need to know about edible berries?" asked Tanya. "In New York we get berries all year round from the vegetable stand on the corner."

"Well, there are no vegetable stands in the wilderness," warned Missy. "You'd better pay attention."

Tanya looked as if she couldn't care less.

CHAPTER

9

"Today's the day," shouted Missy when she woke up. The rest of her tentmates were equally excited. Everyone except Tanya was looking forward to the scavenger hunt.

"Maybe I should pretend to be sick," said Tanya as she got dressed.

"Are you kidding? This is the greatest day of camp," said Missy.

"What's so great about getting to tramp through the woods with no food?"

"It's exciting," said Missy.

Tanya put on a pair of shorts and a short top.

"You'd better put on something warmer," said Missy.

"Don't be silly," said Tanya. "If I'm going to be outside all day, at least I can work on my tan."

"You're either going to burn or freeze, and don't forget the mosquitoes," said Missy. "It can

get cold in the woods, and we're not supposed to take a backpack, just the clothes we wear." Missy had on a T-shirt, a long-sleeved plaid shirt, and a windbreaker.

"If I run into any mosquitoes, I'm going to point my compass toward the main house and come right back."

"But you won't win that way," said Missy.

"The name of the game today is surviving, not winning," answered Tanya.

"It's both," argued Missy. "You win by using all the survival skills we've been learning."

"Yeah, and I've learned that I should have stayed in New York."

"Come on," said Missy. "We'll be late for breakfast. That's when they'll announce the partners."

"And you hope I won't be your partner, don't you?" said Tanya.

Missy didn't answer. Tanya flounced out of the tent ahead of the rest of the group.

"I sure hope *I* don't get Tanya as a partner," Stephanie whispered to Missy as they walked to the mess hall.

"Why not?" asked Missy, feeling her heart sink.

"You must be kidding!" exclaimed Stephanie. "She hasn't paid any attention to what we've been learning this week. I intend to win this hunt!"

"I think I'd die if I got her," said Emily. "She'd be my last choice."

"Don't worry," said Willie. "They'll probably stick her with one of the counselors since she's never been to camp before."

Missy felt terrible that nobody wanted Tanya

for a partner. She remembered what her father had said: "Try to help Tanya have a good time, too." She looked over at the table where the counselors sat, and nodded grimly.

"I'll be right back," she told her friends. Then she walked over to the counselors' table.

"Susan," said Missy, "can I talk to you for a minute?"

"What's the problem?" asked Susan.

"Uh . . . I've decided I really want Tanya as my partner," said Missy.

Susan looked surprised. "Well, to tell you the truth, we were going to pair her with a counselor," she said.

"Yes," said Missy. "But everyone knows that's what you do with the rejects."

Susan blushed. "I didn't realize it was so obvious."

"Anyhow," said Missy, "can you put us together?"

Susan smiled at Missy. "That's a really nice thing you're doing."

Missy grimaced. "Yeah, well, families have to stick together, right?"

"Oh, I don't know." Susan grinned. "It depends on the families."

When the names were read out, Missy's friends looked shocked that Missy and Tanya were named as a team. But no one looked as shocked as Tanya.

"Aren't you going to demand a recount?" Tanya asked.

Missy shook her head. "We're a team," she said. "I've got only one demand."

"What's that?" asked Tanya suspiciously.

"That we try to win," said Missy. "You have to promise me."

Tanya laughed. "You really care about this stupid game?" she asked.

"Yes," said Missy. "It's one that I really think we can win."

Tanya looked at her thoughtfully, and for a moment Missy thought she was going to agree. They would be a team and they would really try to win—together.

Then Tanya's expression changed. "Only a real loser would want to win a scavenger hunt," she said with a scowl.

Missy shook her head hopelessly. "Be quiet," she said. "We have to listen to the rules."

The head counselor, Joanne, read off the rules. Each team would be given one compass. "We've checked them all out," said Joanne with a smile. "So no complaints that your compass doesn't work. You each have eight stops. Each clue is clearly marked by a hikers' sign. Does everybody remember what the hikers' sign is? Tanya?"

Tanya's eyes were closed and she lifted her head to the sun.

Slowly Tanya opened her eyes. "Did I hear my name?"

"What is the hikers' sign?" Joanne asked patiently.

"Scorpio?" Tanya asked.

The whole camp giggled.

"Let's hope for your sake that your partner has been paying better attention," said Joanne. "Missy, what will you look for?"

"A pile of three stones, with the middle stone pointing in the direction we're supposed to go for our next clue. Under the rock is a note telling us how many steps till our next clue."

"That's right," said Joanne. "Remember, the object of this hunt is to make yourself at home in the wilderness. We have confidence in all of you. Enjoy yourselves."

Joanne went to each team and handed out the compasses. "I'll take ours," said Missy.

"I think that's a good idea," said Joanne. "Good luck."

Missy knew that with Tanya as her partner, she'd need it.

"I'll be in charge," Missy said to Tanya. "And *we're* going to win."

Missy slung the canteen over her shoulder and marched off toward the woods. She didn't even bother to look back and make sure that her "teammate" was following.

CHAPTER

10

Missy heard a slap. Then another. She turned around. Tanya was following her through the woods, slapping her arms.

"I'm being eaten alive," complained Tanya. "And I'm starving."

"You shouldn't have eaten your candy bar right away," said Missy. "I warned you." Missy was definitely in control. They had already uncovered four of the eight clues. And they had found their clues in the exact number of steps, so Missy knew she was doing it right. She was pretty sure they were ahead of the other teams.

"We've got only another forty steps to go, and we'll find our fifth clue," she told Tanya.

"Where are we?" complained Tanya. She had done nothing but complain. She wouldn't help Missy count steps or help look for the hikers' signs. As far as Missy was concerned, Tanya was nothing but a royal pain in the neck.

"Why couldn't that last clue have taken us to the lake?" complained Tanya. "I saw some of the other teams go in that direction. Then I could just lie down on the dock."

"Each team starts out in a different direction. If you had paid attention when the rules were read—instead of sticking your stupid face in the sun—you would have known. And we have to stick together in order to win," said Missy.

"I'll meet you at the finish line," said Tanya.

"You dumb jerk. You don't know where the finish line is!" shouted Missy.

"Who are you calling a dumb jerk?" Tanya demanded.

"You!" Missy yelled. "You drive me crazy!"

"Then why did you ask to be my partner?" Tanya asked.

"Because you would have gotten stuck with a counselor if I hadn't!" Missy blurted out.

Tanya slapped at another mosquito. "Give me the compass," she said in a grim voice.

"No," said Missy. Then she paused. "Look, Tanya, I'm sorry I said that. Let's go. We must be near the next hikers' sign. It should be straight ahead. We'll get our next clue. If we work together, we could really win."

"Give me the compass," repeated Tanya.

"Why do you want it?" Missy asked suspiciously.

"I don't want to depend on you for *anything*," said Tanya.

"I told you I was sorry. Can't we forget it?"

"I want the compass," Tanya said angrily.

"We'll share it," said Missy, a little bit scared of Tanya's temper. "You can use it for the last clues."

"I want it *now*," insisted Tanya.

"We've got to act like a team. We're losing time by arguing," said Missy.

Missy had continued to walk as they talked, silently mouthing off the steps so she wouldn't lose count. Suddenly she pointed to a pile of rocks up ahead. "Look!" she cried. "Our next clue!" She turned her back on Tanya and ran to the hikers' sign.

Missy put the compass down on the ground and turned over the rocks. She pulled out a piece of paper. "Five hundred and fifty steps, south by southwest," read Missy.

"Hey!" Missy shouted as Tanya reached down and grabbed the compass.

"You can go south by southwest," said Tanya. "I'm going back."

"You can't. We'll lose," wailed Missy.

"You don't need me as a partner. And you don't need a compass either. You've got a great sense of direction, remember? You've been bragging about it ever since I met you." Tanya peered at the compass, seemed to study it, then tucked it into the pocket of her shorts and headed back in the direction they had come.

Missy jumped up. "You're not going anywhere," she said. "And certainly not with my compass."

Tanya turned around. "Try and stop me," she taunted as she started to walk away.

Missy lunged at Tanya, grabbing her around the waist. They both fell to the ground.

Then they heard it—a horrible crunching sound. Tanya had fallen on the compass.

Missy rolled away onto a pile of leaves. "Was that what I thought it was?" she asked in a horrified voice.

Tanya stood up. She and Missy looked at the ground.

The compass was shattered. The needle was bent in the middle.

Missy picked it up. "You broke the compass!" she said in a hushed voice.

"If you hadn't tackled me, this would never have happened," insisted Tanya. "It's *your* fault!"

Missy held the ruined compass in her hand. She shook it. It rattled. "It's definitely broken." Missy sighed. "Come on, we have to stop fighting and figure out what to do."

"I know what to do—go back," said Tanya. "That's what I wanted to do hours ago."

"Sure, but which way!" said Missy. "We've made so many twists and turns, I'm not sure how to get back to camp. I think we should try to retrace our steps."

"You're nuts," said Tanya. "That will take hours."

"But it's the safer way," pleaded Missy. "Otherwise we could *really* get lost. These woods go on for miles."

"You're just a scaredy cat," said Tanya scornfully. "You always think the worst. I know exactly where camp is. It's right over that hill."

Tanya pointed to a hill that didn't look very far away.

"It's getting late in the afternoon," said Missy. "Maybe they'll come out looking for us. They say that when you get lost, you should stay put."

The sun was already so low in the sky, there were deep shadows everywhere.

"I'm not scared," said Tanya. "And I don't care what they say. *I* say that camp is right over that hill, and that's where I'm going. You've been bossy all day and look where it's gotten us. Lost, with no compass. From now on, I'm taking control."

Tanya plowed forward. Missy followed her. She had to admit that Tanya did have a point. Maybe if Missy hadn't wanted to win so badly, they would never have gotten into this mess.

At first, they followed a little deer trail up the hill, but it stopped at a small clearing. Tanya's arms were scratched from the brambles, and they were no closer to the top of the hill. It was much farther away than either of them had realized.

Tanya looked close to tears. "Where are we?" she cried.

"I think we should stay here," said Missy. She took out the canteen and handed it to Tanya. "Take just a sip. It may have to last us a long time."

Tanya held the canteen and took a long swallow. For a second Missy was scared that Tanya was going to drink all the water. Tanya saw Missy staring at her. She stopped drinking and handed the canteen back to Missy.

"You take a sip," said Tanya softly. "You need water too."

CHAPTER

11

"**I**'m starving," complained Tanya.

"Don't think about it," said Missy. She was scared. The sun had almost set, and Missy knew it would be pitch-dark soon. If nobody found them, they'd probably have to spend the night in the woods.

Missy gathered up some underbrush. Tanya sat huddled with her arms around her knees. Her hair was a matted mess. "What are you doing?" Tanya asked. Her voice sounded tired.

"I've got matches. I'm going to make a fire. We'll feel better when we've got a fire. Maybe somebody will see it. Besides, you must be freezing."

Tanya's arms were full of goose bumps. "Are you going to tell me I told you so?" asked Tanya.

"No," said Missy. "Here, take my jacket. I've got my long-sleeved shirt."

Missy took off her jacket and draped it around

Tanya's shoulders. Missy could see that Tanya was shivering.

"Come on, help me make a fire. That'll keep you warm."

Missy gathered some more kindling and then made a tepee out of sticks. She had a pile of larger sticks nearby. Missy struck a match, and the fire started.

"One match!" said Missy. "That's a record for me. I usually go through about ten."

"Good for you," said Tanya, but she didn't sound sarcastic.

"Come on," said Missy. "Move a little closer to the fire." She put some sticks on the fire. Tanya looked up at the little bit of sky they could see through the tall trees. The sky had turned a purple-velvet color.

"Do you think we're going to be here all night?" Tanya asked.

Missy didn't answer right away. She dug into her pockets. "Aha!" she exclaimed. "I knew I had it." She pulled out half a candy bar.

"We won't starve," said Missy. She cut off a little bit of the candy bar and handed it to Tanya. "Eat this. It will make you feel better. Did you know you can survive for weeks without food as long as you have water?"

Tanya ate the tiny piece of chocolate Missy handed her. "If we eat it in small bites, it'll feel like we're getting a whole meal," said Tanya.

"It's delicious," said Missy, savoring the chocolate as it melted in her mouth.

Tanya rubbed her tummy. "I'm full," she said. "What an enormous meal! I'm going to get fat!"

Missy laughed. Carefully she rewrapped the chocolate and started to put it in her pocket. Then she held it out to Tanya.

"Do you want to keep this for us?" Missy asked.

Tanya shook her head. "No. Things fall out of my pockets, remember?"

"That was my fault," said Missy. "I should have let you quit. You never wanted to come on this scavenger hunt anyhow."

"Stop saying everything's your fault when you know it's mine," said Tanya.

"Hey, none of this is your fault," said Missy.

"Well, it's not yours either," said Tanya. "Let's not talk about whose fault it is, okay?"

"That's one of the best ideas you've had," said Missy, staring into the flames. She picked up a stick and poked at the fire as they sat quietly.

"Do you really hate it here?" Missy asked.

"I'm being eaten alive, I'm starving, I'm cold, and I'm scared," said Tanya. "Why would I hate it?"

"That's not what I meant," said Missy. "I meant *here*, with me, in Indianapolis."

Tanya didn't look at Missy. Instead, she stared into the fire. "Hate it? You've got to be kidding. Compared to the last few months at home, it's been heaven. You've got the perfect life."

Missy was shocked. "What's so perfect about it?" she asked.

"Well, you and your parents are always fooling around and teasing each other. They love each other. They love you. Everybody loves you. Even that big stupid dog loves you. My mom and dad have both been so messed up about getting divorced, it's been awful at home."

"But your parents still love you," said Missy. "And, anyway, I thought *your* life was perfect. You live in New York. Your mom has a great job. You probably meet lots of glamorous people."

"Yeah, but I'd trade it all if my parents would get back together." Tanya sighed.

"Maybe they will," said Missy.

Tanya shook her head. "Take it from me, Missy. *You've* got the perfect life."

Missy laughed.

"Are you laughing at me?" Tanya asked, looking down at the ground.

"No . . . no," said Missy quickly. "I just never thought of *my* life as perfect."

Tanya glanced at Missy. "Because you were adopted?" Tanya looked guilty. "Whoops, I'm sorry. I shouldn't have said that. Mom said I shouldn't talk about it."

"But that's what I hate," said Missy. "People think about it, but they don't talk about it."

"Maybe they're afraid of making you feel uncomfortable," Tanya suggested.

"But I'm not uncomfortable. Being adopted is a part of me," Missy said. "If people would just talk to me about it, they'd know that. I really love my parents—and they love me. But it would be nice to have someone my own age to talk to about it, 'cause sometimes I feel different."

The fire crackled.

"*Everyone* feels different sometimes," said Tanya. "I feel different when I'm around you and your parents."

"You don't have to feel that way," said Missy. "Just give us a chance."

Tanya stared into the fire again.

"After all," said Missy, "you're family, remember?"

Missy placed another large stick in the flames. Tanya scrunched over and sat beside her. The next thing they knew, they were both asleep, side by side, in the cold.

CHAPTER

12

Missy lifted her head. Pink streaks lit up the sky. She felt cold and stiff from sleeping on the ground. Tanya groaned as she rolled over. Her eyes opened.

"I kept waking up all night," said Tanya. "I was sure that hoot owl was going to eat us for supper."

"What hoot owl?" asked Missy.

"You slept through it all," said Tanya. She stood up and brushed herself off. "So much for being rescued," she said.

"I'm sure they're looking for us," said Missy.

"What do you think we should do?" Tanya asked.

Missy smiled at her. Tanya was actually asking her advice, not sarcastically, but as a friend. The only problem was that Missy wasn't sure what they should do. She noticed that their fire was out.

Missy dug into her pocket for the last of their

candy bar. "Breakfast?" she said. She broke the last piece into two even parts.

"I'll never make fun of camp food again," said Tanya.

"We should gather wood for a big fire," said Missy. "I still think that's our best hope of being seen. I'll go look for some wood. We've used up all the big pieces around here."

"I'll help," said Tanya. "You're not leaving me alone."

"Okay," said Missy. "Let's go." They had gone only a couple of yards back into the forest when suddenly they heard a loud rustling noise.

"What's that?" Tanya asked, grabbing Missy's arm.

Missy stood completely still. She could hear twigs breaking. "It sounds like an animal," she whispered.

"It sounds like a *big* animal," Tanya whispered back.

Tanya and Missy huddled together as the noises came closer.

"Are there any bears in these woods?" Tanya said in a tiny voice.

Missy nodded slowly. "These woods are full of bears," she squeaked. "I didn't want to tell you before. I was afraid you'd be scared."

"What do you think I am now?" hissed Tanya.

"I'm scared too," whispered Missy. She hugged Tanya and shut her eyes. Maybe if they were as still as statues, the bear wouldn't notice them.

The sounds grew closer. "It sounds huge," whispered Missy.

"It *is* a bear!" screamed Tanya, as she broke away. *"Run, Missy, run!"*

Missy didn't run. She jumped straight into the air, grabbing hold of a tree branch. Pulling herself up into the tree, she looked down to see Tanya trip over a root and flop over. She lay where she fell, frozen in fear.

Something large and hairy and with four big feet broke through the underbrush. It leaped on Tanya and started to lick her face.

"*Baby*!" screamed Missy. Baby kept jumping on Tanya, kissing her all over.

"Tanya! It's *Baby*. He found us. We're rescued. My folks must have heard we were lost. They brought Baby! He'll lead us back."

But Tanya was curled into a little ball, looking more scared than ever.

Missy started climbing down. As soon as Baby spotted her, he jumped up on the trunk of the tree, then jumped back to Tanya, barking.

"Get him away from me," Tanya begged tearfully. "Please, Missy."

"But it's Baby, not a bear," said Missy. "Come on, get up."

"I can't," said Tanya. "I'm even more scared of dogs than I am of getting lost again."

Missy stared at Tanya in disbelief. Then she grabbed Baby's collar. "I'll hold him. You can get up now."

Missy pulled Baby to the other side of the clearing. Tearfully Tanya got to her feet. She stood with her back to the tree, shaking.

"You're scared of Baby?" Missy asked.

"I was afraid to tell you," said Tanya. "I thought you'd call *me* a baby."

"But Baby won't hurt you."

"I hate big dogs," said Tanya. "Once I got bitten by a dog who looked just like Baby on the set of one of Mom's commercials."

"Is that why you locked Baby in the basement that night?" Missy asked.

Tanya nodded. "I'm sorry. But I was afraid to have him in the room with me."

"You should have told me," said Missy. "I would have understood."

"But you loved Baby so much. I thought you'd hate anybody who didn't love your dog. I thought you'd hate *me*, so I made sure you didn't like me anyhow." She looked at Baby. "I bet he hates me. I'm surprised he didn't bite me when he had the chance."

"Baby wouldn't bite," said Missy. "He likes you. Here, I'll show you. I'll hold him, and you give him a pat."

Tanya swallowed hard. "Come on," said Missy. "After all, he *did* rescue us!"

"I—I guess so," Tanya said. "I shouldn't be afraid after all we've been through."

With a deep breath Tanya took a step forward, and then another. Baby wagged his tail. Slowly Tanya put out her hand. Baby licked it. Tanya laughed.

"He tickles."

Just then Missy heard a voice. "*Missy! Tanya!*"

"That's Mom!" shouted Missy. "Mom, Dad, here we are!"

Seconds later Mr. and Mrs. Fremont crashed through the woods. They were followed by Susan and Joanne. Mrs. Fremont ran to Missy and Tanya and swept them both into her arms.

"I was so worried," said Mrs. Fremont. "About both of you."

"We were all worried," said Joanne.

"We broke our compass," explained Missy.

"But Missy knew all about survival in the woods," said Tanya quickly. "We built a fire. She was great."

Mr. Fremont hugged Tanya and Missy tightly. "What a terrible experience for you," he said.

Tanya looked at Missy. "Oh, it wasn't so bad."

"We'll get you back to camp and cleaned up," said Mr. Fremont. "And then we'll get Tanya back home."

"Home?" said Missy. "We still have two days of camp left!" She and Tanya looked at each other. "You can't break up a great team."

"You really want to stay?" Mrs. Fremont asked.

Tanya looked from Missy to Baby. "Definitely," she said. "Not many people can say their cousin is also their best friend."

"How about the best friend's dog?" Missy asked, smiling at Tanya.

"I guess he's a best friend too." Tanya laughed. She and Missy winked at each other and, arm in arm, headed back to camp together, with Baby bounding along beside them.